And the Story Continues

By:
Xiomara Rodriguez

Copyright © 2023 by Xiomara Rodriguez

ISBN: 978-1-77883-061-7 (Paperback)

978-1-77883-062-4 (E-book)

All rights reserved. No part of this publication may be reproduced, distributed, or transmitted in any form or by any means, including photocopying, recording, or other electronic or mechanical methods, without the prior written permission of the publisher, except in the case brief quotations embodied in critical reviews and other noncommercial uses permitted by copyright law.

The views expressed in this book are solely those of the author and do not necessarily reflect the views of the publisher, and the publisher hereby disclaims any responsibility for them.

BookSide Press
877-741-8091
www.booksidepress.com
orders@booksidepress.com

CONTENTS

Dedication v
Foreword vii
Chapter 1: A New Day 1
Chapter 2: A Night For All Nights 9
Chapter 3: The Next Day 15
Chapter 4: The Investigation 23
Chapter 5: The Funeral 33
Chapter 6: The Investigation Continues 37
Chapter 8: The FBI 49
Chapter 9: TOM? 61
Chapter 10: The End, Maybe? 69

DEDICATION

I dedicate this book, not only to my family that have always supported me, my husband, who is always there for me, but to two very dear friends, Kyle Waxman, and Marsy Kupersmith. Without their help, this book would not have been possible.

Thank you all.
Xiomara Rodriguez

FOREWORD

I know I've said this before, but I'll say it again. The author of this book is a brilliant, strong, intelligent, beautiful woman who is capable of anything. She also happens to be my loving wife of 40 years. That said, in her first book, "How Could It Be", she introduced you to Jane Sparks, a crime solving detective with the San Francisco Police Department. In this, her second book, she weaves a fast-paced mystery with many twists and turns. The story and characters will keep you glued to the pages until the very end. I hope you enjoy it as much as I did.

David Wolfe

CHAPTER 1

A New Day

It had been sometime since I was promoted to Chief of Detectives. At first the promotion seemed great, but the truth is that it is not all that is meant to be. The politics of this job are endless. I have to deal with such BS that is not even funny. Sometimes I wish I was back to being an Inspector. But there is no turning back, and I try to make the best of each day.

I still keep a close tie with Peterson. She is outstanding and a very trustworthy person. On the other hand, I really don't trust the new Homicide Lieutenant. There is something about him that I really don't like.

He is always so ready to please me. It's like having a puppy who needs attention constantly, but at the same time, he is ready to bite you.

But, as I am drinking my coffee, I put all those thoughts away. The day here in San Francisco woke up so beautiful. It is a shame to deny myself such a beautiful day, with thoughts of things I truly cannot change.

But that was going to change for me, like it or not with a call from Peterson.

--"Chief," she said, "a body was discovered at the 2nd

level of the parking garage at SFHQ. I needed you to be aware of this because it's going to be all over the news in a short time."

--"I'm on my way, but I need all the information you have," I said as I put down my coffee and headed out the door.

--"According to his ID, his name is Jonny Price. He spells his name J-o-n-n-y, which is not a common spelling for the name. He was found dead at the entrance of the second level of the parking garage. He was shot twice in the head and the body dumped there. According to the Medical Examiner, it seems like he has been dead for a few hours. I have no other information for you this time. It seemed like he worked for a local horse stable. Do you think his death could open that horse smuggling case again?" she said. I could hear in her voice that there was something else she just did not want to say.

--"Thank you. I will be at my office shortly to deal with this. See you when I get in. If anything changes, please let me know, and please be discreet about it," I said as I hung up the phone.

I had just finished my conversation with Peterson when I got a call from Claire, our Medical Examiner, telling me that Jonny Price's body was in her morgue, that he had been shot twice in the back of the head and, according to the body temperature, he had been dead for at least 6 hours, but she will know more about it once she completed her autopsy.

And still no call from LT Parks about the body and what was going on. But I will give him a chance.

I arrived at SFHQ in record time and headed straight to my office. Waiting for me there was Paul Johnson, Chief of the Media Relations Unit. He did not seem incredibly happy. I did not have to wait too long to find out what was upsetting him.

--"You need to do something with your LT. Put a muzzle on him. He has just gone over my head and is setting up a press conference regarding the body they just found in our parking garage. He is out of order and out of place. Dealing with the press is my job, not his. If he wants to be in front of the camera, he can transfer to our division or go and be a reporter for one of the local stations," he said in a truly angry tone.

--"Paul, please calm down and tell me what is going on," I said in my best soothing voice possible, because like Paul, I was boiling with anger inside. How dare him.

Paul explained that a body of a man had been found in the second level of our parking garage. The full autopsy had not yet been performed. It was believed the deceased was Jonny Price. He had been a stable hand at the SFPD Mounted Unit. There was no more information at the time, but because the body was found on the 2nd floor of the parking garage, and because the shooting of an FBI Agent had also happened in our parking garage, the press was all over it.

He also stated that he did not need some hotshot LT calling a press conference when we still do not have all the info, or at least no official statement has been made.

I assured Paul that I was going to take care of it, and that seemed to calm him somewhat.

As he was about to leave my office he said, "It was so much easier working with you when you were a LT, but things change, don't they." And he left my office.

It took all I had to control myself. I called LT Parks to my office. It took him forever to get to my office.

--"Could you tell me why you did not call me when a body was found in our 2nd floor parking garage. Why did I have to find out from Chief of the Media Relations Unit," I said in a very harsh tone.

--"Chief, I was going to call you..."

I interrupted, "When? When the press was in your office? When things like this happen, I AM THE FIRST PERSON YOU CALL. YOU DO NOT TAKE IT UPON YOURSELF TO CALL A PRESS CONFERENCE. That job is for the Media Relations Unit. Do I make myself clear? Now I need to know what is going on," I said in a very demanding tone

As I sat down, LT Parks was about to sit when I said, "No, don't sit, just tell me. This is not a friendly meeting"

He looked at me with contempt and a bit of surprise. I don't think he likes the idea of being told what to do by a woman.

"Also, I want the best Inspector you have on this case, which is Peterson and her partner, Martinez. They will report directly to me..."

Parks interrupted, "But I am their direct supervisor, you can't do that," he said in an angry tone.

--"Yes, I can, and I am doing it. And if I find out you have gone over my head and the Chief of the Media Relations Unit's head, I will bring you up on charges for disobeying a direct order. DO I MAKE MYSELF CLEAR. Now please leave my office and be so kind as to send in Peterson and her partner. I need to call the Chief of Police."

LT Parks left my office and minutes later Peterson and Martinez walked in.

--"Chief, you wanted to see us?" Peterson said.

I was on the phone with the Chief of Police when Peterson and Martinez came to my office. I motioned them to sit and I continued my conversation with the Chief.

--"I will keep you updated. Yes sir, we cannot continue to have dead bodies showing up in our parking garage. Yes sir, I have the best inspector handling this matter. Yes sir, LT

Parks has been advised that he is not to conduct any press or give interviews about this case or any case without the approval of the Chief of the Media Relations Unit. Yes sir, I do understand how upset Paul is. I will make sure this never happens again. Thank you, Sir."

After my conversation with the Chief of Police, I was even more upset.

--"I don't know if LT Parks told you, but you are going to be handling the Jonny Price case. You will report directly to me. I will keep LT Parks up to date, as well as the Chief and the Media Unit. I know that this is not the way the chain of command goes, but in this case, this is the way it is going to work. You will run everything by me. YOU WILL NOT SPEAK TO THE MEADIA ABOUT THIS CASE. YOU WILL HANDLE THIS CASE BY THE BOOK. Is that understood? Now tell me where we are at this time."

Peterson updated me on all that was going on. When she was in the middle of her report, Claire walked in with more information.

--"Jonny Price was not killed where we found him. As I told you before he was shot twice at close range in the back of the head. The weapon was a .380 automatic. Ballistics believes it is from a Walther PPK. He was shot execution style. But the ammo in this case seems to be made, not store brought. Also, we do not have the results of the toxicology report, and the Crime Scene Unit is working on the trace evidence on the plastic tarp that he was wrapped in. There is evidence that he was tortured prior to getting killed. Two fingers on the right and three on the left hand were broken. He must have been in a lot of pain when he was shot. As soon as I get more info, I will let you know," Claire said.

--"Peterson, how did you guys identify him, by his fingerprints?"

--"No, he had his wallet, money and his watch. What was remarkably interesting was a note that we found attached to his shirt, "Uoytogi". It reminded me of the other case," she said.

--"Claire when you finish with the full autopsy and get the trace and toxicology report, please let me know the findings. For full disclosure, I have known Price for a long time. He used to be a stable hand at the SFPD Mounted Police Unit when I was a member. He used to take care of my horse. He was fired when he tested positive for drugs. He was a good guy. He just could not catch a break. Remember, I need this done by the book. I need to know who did this. Last time I spoke to Price, he was going to get a job at Monroe Stables and Training. Peterson, you and Martinez do a full background on him. Get a search warrant for his room at the stables, as wells as the stalls of the horses he was attending to. It should be about three. Also, the tack room and the trainer's office. That will be all for now, thanks," I said with some sadness in my voice.

--"We understand Chief," Peterson said, and they all left my office.

As they were leaving my phone rang.

--"Hi Fran, how are you doing? I was wondering how long it was going to take for you to call," I said, "No, this is not going to be a case that needs FBI assistance. Fran, I am ok, I am a big girl, and believe it or not, I can handle myself. All is well, how is Sasha doing? How about if we all have dinner at my house tonight. Yes, I will order some Puerto Rican food. How about 8ish.? Yes, Fran I am ok. See you tonight." And with that my conversation with my sister ended.

The rest of the day went extremely slow. More reports continued to come in about Price. Paul, along with LT Parks, conducted a press conference. I had decided not to be part of it. I hate press conferences, so I told LT Parks to handle it. He seemed to be in his element, and he stayed on script. I just could not wait for this day to be over.

CHAPTER 2

A Night For All Nights

As I promised my sister and her wife, I ordered the Puerto Rican food, and picked it up on my way home, along with a bottle of wine. The day had not been a good day. I felt so sad about the death of Jonny Price. He was a good man who faced many challenges in life and tried extremely hard to survive them all. I really hoped that the night with my sister and her wife would be bring some solace to my hurting heart.

Around 7:30 pm Fran and Sasha rang the doorbell, and to my surprise, Sasha had an exceptionally beautiful bouquet of flowers.

--"Hi guys, come in, and you did not have to bring me flowers. They are beautiful, hibiscus right," I said in a surprised tone.

--"We did not get you flowers, this were outside when we got here," Fran said.

--Well, who could have sent them? Let me see the card," I said.

I took the card and it read, "Best of luck, you will need it: Jonny."

--"Jonny sent these flowers, but when? We found him dead today. When did he send them?" I questioned.

--"Is there a name of the florist in the card? You can call them tomorrow to find out when the order was placed. Also, the location of the flower shop. That might give you an idea where he was before he was killed," Sasha said, looking intensively at the flowers.

--"What do you know about hibiscus?" Sasha asked.

--"Nothing," I said, as I placed the flowers on the dining room table, "But they are beautiful, even though I like tulips better, but these are good. I love the colors. He sent a dozen of them, all different colors."

By this time, Fran had taken the food out of the containers, had set plates out and was urging us to get started with the eating. When it came to Puerto Rican food, Fran was ready at any time and today was no exception.

We served ourselves and sat down with good wine. I was hoping for an enjoyable conversation that was not work related, but that was not going to happen.

--"So how did you meet Jonny Price?" Fran asked.

--"He was the groom that handled my horse when I was in the Mounted Unit," I answered in an incredibly sad tone.

--"Was that all?" Fran asked again.

--"What do you mean, if that was all?" I asked.

--"You know what I mean," she said.

--Yes, I know what you meant, but there was nothing more than just a friendship," I replied.

As we ate, I told them how I had met Jonny, how great he was with my horse and how much care he put into taking care not only of my horse, but the other horses that he tended to. I told them how sad I was when I found out he tested positive in a drug test and that he was fired from the Unit.

I also told them how he went down the wrong path with drugs and that one day he showed up at my office asking for help. He had no family, so I helped him get into rehab. When he got out, he promised not to use again. But that did not last long, and once again I helped him. I told him that was going to be the last time, and he promised.

I explained that about two months ago, I got a call from Jonny. He told me that he was clean and sober, and that he was getting a job at the Monroe Stables and Training, the same place where Dorothy had also worked as a stale hand. This was too much of a coincidence.

I continued with my story. I asked him if he could keep an eye on things and if he saw something that he considered out of place, to give me call or send me a message.

--"So, he was your Confidential Informant?" Fran interrupted.

--"Yes and no. I am still intrigued at what is going on out there, but I don't have enough evidence that a crime is being committed. After the Chief took her life, the case of the smuggled horses basically died with her. But it did not for me. You were shot and I was stabbed, which is personal, and I need to finish what they started. Whoever they are," I said, a bit irritated.

--"Ok, I am there with you. This is personal for me too, so let's try to figure out what is going on," Fran said.

As we were talking, Sasha was taking a close look at the flowers that I had just received.

--"Did you know that Hibiscus are native to warm temperate, subtropical and tropical regions throughout the world. Member species are renowned for their large, showy flowers. Also, a tea made from hibiscus flowers is known by many names around the world and is served both hot and cold. The beverage is known for its red color, tart flavor, and vitamin C content," Sasha said as she continued to look at the flowers.

--By "the way you have purple flowers that mean mystery, yellow ones that mean good fortune and white ones that mean beauty. I think he was sending you a message, maybe "beautiful, good fortune solving your mystery," Sasha continued.

--"Leave it to the writer in the room to come up with such an idea," Fran said with a laugh.

--"No, maybe she is onto something. Maybe he could not get the information to me for fear that he could be followed, so he sends it in a very discreet way," I said.

--"Yeah, but he still got killed," Fran said.

--"You know you might be right. There are a number of different flowers of different colors. There are five purple flowers, which mean mystery, four white ones for beauty and 3 yellow ones for good luck. I think he really was trying to tell you something," Sasha said.

--"Like what?" I asked.

--"Is there a Hibiscus Street in San Francisco?" Sasha asked.

We all search for the answer on our Wi-Fi, and yes, there is a Hibiscus Drive in San Francisco.

--"Could you see if there is a 534 Hibiscus Drive or Street?" Sasha asked.

--"There is a Hibiscus Drive and it is a very short street. It seems to be a residential area and yes, it looks like there is a 534," I said.

--"Well, your next stop should be 534 Hibiscus Drive," Sasha said.

--"This is like a scavenger hunt. I'm in," Fran said

--"So am I. We will take a look at 534 Hibiscus Drive in

the morning. Now let's enjoy the food and the wine," I said.

As we were settling down for our meal, a knock on the door startled us.

--"Are you waiting for someone else?" Fran asked.

--"I have no idea who it could be," I said as I walked toward the door. To my surprise it was Tom. It was a month since the last time I saw him.

--"Hi, come in. We were just sitting down for dinner. What brings you by?" I asked.

--"I heard that they had found a body at SFPDHQ and I was wondering how you were doing," he said.

--"All is well," I said, "please come in and join us for dinner."

Tom did join us, but we did not touch on Jonny and that he was the body at SFPDHQ and that I had received the flowers from him. However, Tom was asking lots of questions about the murder, the body, who could it be and who the flowers were from.

It was about 10:00pm when Tom left. His visit just felt strange to all. Not much later after Tom left and after helping me pick up things, Sasha and Fran also left. Let's see what tomorrow brings, I said to myself.

The night seemed strange, and I felt a deep sorrow in my heart. Someone I knew was murdered and his body was left at the steps of the building where I worked. I received flowers from this same dead man the day he was found dead. The flowers created a small scavenger hunt. My ex-husband shows up at my doorstep unexpectedly. Yes, this was really a night for all nights.

As I got ready for bed, I wondered what tomorrow will bring.

CHAPTER 3

The Next Day

It was an exceptionally beautiful San Francisco day, like normal. I was having my morning coffee, my black morning coffee. I am not one of those people that adds tons of stuff to my coffee. And to be very sincere, I will have iced coffee when pigs fly.

And as I was drinking my coffee and reading my newspaper, I heard a knock on my door and the door opened. It was Fran and Sasha, as agreed.

A while back I had given Fran a copy of my house key, in case of an emergency, so she and Sasha came in and they shared a cup of coffee with me and after the coffee, we all left for 534 Hibiscus Drive.

I was wondering what we would find there. I tried extremely hard not to have any expectations, but what I expected, and the reality of things were two different things.

As Fran, Sasha and I approached 534 Hibiscus Drive, it was a residential area, as we thought. We were stunned to see a lot of police presence at the house, the front door was open. As we approached, we were stopped by an officer and after we showed our ID's, we were able to cross the crime scene tape.

As we entered, it was apparent that the place had been ransacked, as if someone was looking for something. Fran and I walked farther into the house and there, in the middle of the floor of the living room, was a body. And he looked very dead.

I was about to call Peterson and Martinez and advise them of the situation when they walked in. I was not surprised to see them.

--"What is going on?" I asked.

--"The wife found the body when she came back from Yoga class," Peterson said, "The wife goes to yoga every Tuesday at 8:00am and returns at about 9:15," she continued. "When she got home the door was open and she found her husband dead. She called the police, they called me. I was about to call you when I saw you. I also called Claire and asked her to please come with the Crime Scene Unit Team."

--"By the way, who called you?" she asked.

--"It's a long story. I will update you a bit later. Was this a robbery gone bad or was this deliberate?" I asked.

--"It looks like it was deliberate. He has been shot twice to the back of the head, just like Jonny Price. And it seems as if whoever killed him was looking for something," she said.

The pressing question was: Who knew about this place? Had someone followed Jonny? What were they looking for? Did they find it? Did someone know that I was coming to this location? If they knew, how and when did they find out?

Claire said she estimated that the man had been dead for about an hour. She determined that he was kneeling when he was shot, that he was shot where we found the body due to the blood splatter. According to the ID in his wallet, he was Nargial Brookes, the resident of the house. According to the information provided to the police by his wife, he is the owner of a small art gallery in San Francisco.

It seemed that Brookes had been killed a little before Fran, Sasha and I left my house.

But what were they looking for, and why was this man dead?

Outside the fact that he was shot twice to the back of the head, Claire would not tell me anything else until she did a full autopsy. One thing I was sure of was that the bullets in the back of the head had a lot to do with it. Meanwhile the Crime Scene Unit Team was processing the scene very thoroughly.

The house was fairly large. It looked like it was a four-bedroom house, with two and a half bathrooms, a full dining room, a large kitchen, a family room, and a fairly large living room. There was some expensive art on the walls, or at least the art that was not on the floor slashed, as if someone was looking for something in particular. But what was it, what did they think was hidden in this house? What?

At back of the house there was a small shed, and a back door was open. And again, the shed was trashed, but it seemed like whoever was there did not have enough time to go through the shed. When did they leave? Did they leave because they heard the wife arrive? Still, what were they looking for?

As both Fran and I looked around, Sasha had joined Claire in examining the body. A Crime Scene Unit Tech approached me and we followed him to the back of the shed. Tucked behind some old junk, there was something that looked like a package. As he pulled it out, there, in big black letters, was my name.

--"This is addressed to you, what do you want done?" the Tech asked.

--"Make sure you take pictures of it and where you

found it, then tag it and take it to the lab. Make sure you follow all the procedures; I don't want anything questioned later. Keep Peterson and Martinez informed of everything," I said.

Peterson and Martinez knew to keep me updated of what was going on. Fran and I left the crime scene, and Sasha stayed with Claire. Once a medical examiner, always a medical examiner.

Instead of going directly to my office, Fran and I stopped at a small coffee shop close by for something to eat.

--"What are you thinking?" Fran asked.

--"I find all this very puzzling and disturbing. First someone I know is found dead at the steps of the SFPDHQ. Then on the same day that he is found dead I get flowers from him. We play a guessing game and come up with this address. When we get here, we find another dead body, a package that could be a painting addressed to me. But who knew, outside of us three, that we were coming here? We did not even mention that to Tom last night. If I was paranoid, I would say that my house was bugged," I stated.

--"That does not sound to paranoid to me. I was just thinking the same thing," she said.

--"Do you know someone that can check to make sure my house and even your house are not bugged?" I asked.

--"As a matter of fact, yes, I do. I will get in touch with them and I will set things for as soon as possible," Fran said, "Maybe it is not the house. Maybe it was the flowers that you got yesterday. There might be a bug in them."

She looked at me and then continued, "I was reading the other day that a foreign government had developed a system that they could use to hack your cell phone and be able to hear all that goes on and even watch what is going on around you, wherever your phone is. Maybe that is how they found out about what we were planning to do."

--"But that system cannot be cheap. Whoever is behind this has to have a lot of money or some really good connections," I said.

--"You are right, but who?" she said.

Before we left the coffee shop, I called Peterson to ask her if she had gotten the search warrant for Jonny's case, the trainer's office, and the tack area where the saddles and riding equipment were kept. Another thing that I needed her to do was to do a full background check on the owners of the stables. We needed to know everything about them. I also asked her to get all the information on Mr. Brookes.

Before we left the coffee shop, I explained to Fran that grooms live on the back stretch - they have buildings with rooms for them near the stables (actually, the building looks like a converted barn) so they can get to their horses quickly and early in the morning. So we have to get a warrant, not only for his room, but also for the stables that he managed.

I dropped Fran at her office, and then went straight to my office.

When I got to my office, I was greeted by chaos. Once again, the Chief of the Media Relations Unit was in my office waiting for me. Once again Parks had tried to go over the Chief of the Media Relations Unit and that was not setting well with him. I was told that either I keep my boy on a short leash, or he was going to have to act on the matter.

There were several calls from the Chief of Police wanting to know if these cases were related and why there was a package with my name on it at the crime scene.

After a lengthy conversation with the Chief, and an even longer conversation with Parks, I was exhausted. I really could use a long run, nachos, and a beer. But all that would have to wait, as I was called by Claire to go down to the

Crime Lab.

--"What's up?" I asked as I walked in.

--"We x-rayed the package, and it seems that there was a letter inside, in addition to a painting. We opened it and guess what the painting is. It's a painting of you when you were in the Mounted Unit and the letter was addressed to you."

--"Did you open the letter?" I asked.

--"No, we were waiting for you," Claire said.

--"I am here. What are we waiting for? And I see that you dusted it for prints. Did you find anything interesting with the prints?" I said.

-- "The only prints were of our victim. We also found our victim's fingerprints in the Hibiscus Drive house. It seems that he had visited that house several times. Now let's take a look at the letter," she said.

I opened the envelope very carefully and opened the letter:

> My dear and beautiful friend:
>   If you are reading this, it means I am gone. I need to thank you for all you have done for me and your many years for friendship. Thank you, my friend.
> I hope you like the flowers; they led you to this letter. So, it is time to get to the important part:
>   First, when I got to the stables, I began to notice some things that were not right. I brought some of my concerns to the trainer and I was told to mind my business if I knew what was good for me.
> Here are my concerns:
>   A number of horses are sold via private purchases for what I believe is above the true value of the horse. These sales and purchases are for cash, above what

the actual price of the horse could be, but not that high that it would be questioned by authorities. Yes, my friend I believe the horses are dirty money.

I had a two-year-old horse, that I genuinely believed was worth no more than 10 thousand dollars, brought to the stable. This horse was sold to the stable for 20 thousand dollars, double the amount of the horse's worth. Then the horse was insured for the purchase price which the insurance company believed was the legitimate value of the horse and the insurance company did not question the amount.

This horse came from Mexico and we were told it was a great racehorse that had won multiple races. I saw the paperwork and he had all the identifiers that are required. I checked the horse's history, and I did not see anything that told me he was a great racehorse, but all his paperwork at the entry point was correct. So, I believe the horse came into the country legally.

I was put in charge of this horse, and not long after he was in our stable, the horse "gets" a severe case of colic. This is when a horse's bowels tie up or has a lot of gas and because of the way a horse is built internally this can be legitimately fatal. This happened in the middle of the night and by the time I got there, the trainer and the vet had administered to the horse. He became so sick that he had to be put down. I believe an insurance claim was filed.

Not long after my horse had to be put down, another groom has another two-year-old from Mexico. In this case, the horse is cast in his stall. This is when a horse starts trying to climb up the side of the stall and one or both front legs get caught, the horse panics because he can't get down and winds up severely hurting himself to the point of breaking part of a leg. This also happened in the middle of the night and again the trainer comes with a vet even before the groom is called, and they put this horse down.

By this time, I was truly suspicious. I started looking at some of the sales and purchases for horses and I found out that every horse that was brought to the stable from Mexico was sold at a higher price than it was worth. They were insured for the sale value and, shortly after, the horse had to be put down for "legitimate" reasons.

A few of the horses were placed in races where they won and, after a few wins, they were sold for still a higher value of the horse and the horse was gone.

I am in the middle of checking this out, but I am attaching copies of some of the papers I could get. I hope this helps you. I will try to do more, but I think my time is up and I know that this will be our last communication.

Just remember that I am proud to have been your friend and I know that you will not rest until you find my killer and what is going on with this stable.

Please be safe and careful. These people are ruthless; they will not stop for anything.

Bye my friend. I never told you I loved you.

Jonny

After reading the letter, I had tears in my eyes, tears of anger and loss. I had lost a dear friend to a group of ruthless killers who did not stop at killing defenseless animals and people. They needed to be stopped. The question was how?

CHAPTER 4

The Investigation

It had been an awfully long and painful day. All I wanted was to take a long bath, put on my PJ's, sit in front of my TV eating nachos and having a beer.

This was the way I was going to mourn my dear friend. There were so many times that he came to my apartment, and we had nachos and beer, his favorite food. He always said that nachos were the perfect meal. It had all the food groups. I chuckle at the thought. Jonny was a great guy. I had asked him why he spelled his name the way he did and he said that was the way his mother spelled it on his birth certificate. We both laughed about it.

On one occasion, while we were having beers and nachos, he told me he lost his parents in a car crash when he was just 7 years old. He became a ward of the state and was shuffled from foster care to foster care until he ended up in a horse stable. They boarded horses for rich people. He said that it was there where he learned to love and care for horses. But that was also where he learned about drugs. By the time he was 18, he was addicted to marijuana.

In addition to his love for horses, he had seen the SFPD Mounted Unit, and he wanted to join, so he tried extremely hard to stop using, but he failed the entry test. So, he had to settle for being a groom.

All was going well until he had the drug test that ended all his dreams.

Remembering Jonny and his life was really hard, and now I had to work on his funeral. I could not let him be buried in an unmarked grave in Potter's field.

As I wondered what I was going to do for his funeral, I finished my bath, had my pj's on and was working on my nachos, when my phone rang. It was Fran.

--"Hi what are you doing?" she asked.

--"Making some nachos, getting a beer, and I'm going to sit in front of my tv and watch my favorite show. Why?" I asked.

--"What are you watching?" she asked.

--"I am going to watch re-runs of Rizzoli and Isles. Why?" I said.

--"Hey, don't get testy I am just checking on you. Just making sure that you are okay. How about if we have coffee tomorrow. I will text you the address for this great coffee shop, and we can talk," she said as she hanged the phone.

That was a strange call, but I was not in the mood for any calls or any other human, so I did not pay any more attention to my sister's call. I sat with my nachos and my beer to watch one of my favorite shows, hoping for a peaceful night.

I got up early, went for my usual morning run, but today it felt different. It felt like I was being followed, but I just could not pinpoint who and what was following me. I brushed it off as paranoia. Back home, I did my normal morning routine and off I went to meet with my sister.

As I entered the coffee shop, I saw her, she waved at me.

--"Your coffee, black and no sugar. I still can't understand how you can drink it that way," she said.

--"And I cannot understand how you can drink your coffee with so much stuff, is there coffee in there?" I said.

We both laughed and she passed me a note that read, "Your phone has been hacked by a foreign identity. Be careful what you say."

--"So, how is Sasha today?" I asked.

Another note, "I had your phone checked out. Your hackers can hear everything you say at all times and anywhere."

--"She is doing great, having writer's block," she said with a chuckle.

Still another note, "Put your phone on the table next to mine. I need to make a copy of it. When I am finished, turn off your phone."

Within seconds, she synced my phone to her phone. I turned off my phone.

--"Now we can speak freely. Somehow your phone was hacked. Whoever did that has lots of money and connections. The technology used in your phone is very advanced and is only available to foreign countries and special interest groups," she said.

--"How did you find out about it?" I asked.

--"Because mine and Sasha's phones were also hacked. I had one of my techs check my phone out and he found the hack. Then I had him check Sasha's and the same hack was used, so I was sure that your phone was also hacked," she said.

--"But when could that happened?" I asked.

--"At any time. The phone doesn't have to be close to the hacker. As long as they know what they are doing, it is not all that hard. That explains how they knew what we were doing and where we were going when they killed the art gallery owner," she stated.

--"So, we need to find out who is behind all of this," I said.

We sat there a few seconds in silence, as I observed what was going on. Then she asked about Jonny. I told her about the letter, and that I was going to make sure that he had a good funeral.

Once again, we sat in silence. This was a tough time for me, and she truly understood.

--"I will take care of finding out about the hacker and the connections to the stable. You need to find out who killed your friend and the art gallery owner. I am sure there is a connection with those two crimes and maybe to you. I will keep you posted on what is going on at my end; you do the same. And by the way, I will be sending a tech to check your office computer and your laptop. They are both hacked," she said.

She held my hand for a few seconds, then got up to leave, "Please be careful of what you say and do. We don't know who is behind all this, so please be careful. Now turn on your phone and try to act as normal as you can. Whoever is behind all this is extremely dangerous," she said.

I turned on my phone, then we continued a very civil conversation. After a few minutes, she said goodbye, got up and left.

I sat there for a few more minutes as I pondered about all that was going on. A call from Peterson brought me back to the present.

--"Sparks...Yes, I will be at my office in about an hour.... I will see you then..."

This was going to be another exceedingly long day. Peterson had obtained the search warrant needed. Maybe she and Martinez could find something about who and where Jonny was killed. And I still had a funeral to plan.

Before I even got to my office, I got a text from Claire that she wanted to see me as soon as possible.

--"What's up?" I asked.

--"According to the paperwork I just got, you are claiming Jonny Price's body. Are you sure you want to do this?" she asked.

--"Yes, he was a friend. He did not have anyone else. He was a good man that made some really bad choices and, at the end, he wanted to do what he thought was right and that probably was what got him killed," I stated.

--"I hope you understand that whoever killed him will be coming for you for whatever information you might have," she said in a worried tone.

--"Yes, I know, but he needs a proper funeral, and I will give him one," I said, "What else can you tell me regarding his death?" I asked in a very somber tone.

--"We know that his last meal was nachos, lots of jalapeños. From what we can tell, they were homemade. His hands where the hands of a working man. I would say that he spent most of his life around horses. But what surprised me was that there was paint, not house paint, but art paint under his fingernail, in addition to wood splinters, especially his right-hand fingernails. We found traces of an adhesive substance on both his wrists, face, and ankles, which leads me to believe that he was duct taped to the chair. The chair was placed on top of the tarp that we found him in. We could see the indentations of the chair on the trap. The blood spatter on his clothing and the tape lead us to believe that he was sitting on the chair when he was killed, then placed on the tarp for transport. As I told you before, he had some of his fingers broken before he was shot. Regarding drugs, he was clean. He had been clean for some time.

Claire looked at me with concern in her eyes, then said,

"If you really want to do this, I will sign the paperwork and his body will be released to you. Just tell me what funeral home will pick him up. But I still don't approve of this."

--"Could I get back to you on the funeral home. Also, was there any trace of where he might have been killed?" I asked.

--"Yes, oil, like the one you use for saddles. So have Peterson and Martinez take a close look at the tack room," She said, with a worried tone both in her voice and eyes.

Before I went back to my office, I asked her about the body at Hibiscus Drive. She told me she was still working on it and would give me a report later on.

When I got back to my office, my heart was heavy; I needed to make the arrangements. I called the same funeral home I had used for my father's funeral and made all the arrangements.

I had just finished with them, when I was advised that the computer tech was waiting for me. He did not look like any of the techs that I knew, so I thought he was one of Fran's techs.

As I was going to move so he could work, I got a text from Fran advising me that her tech would not be at my office until later that afternoon. I acknowledged her text and told her that I had a computer tech in my office and that I needed to go.

I made no big deal about the guy, and I let him work in the computer. He said he was installing a new anti-virus program and that he would be done shortly. I took a long look at him, and his ID badge so I could talk to the IT director later.

Like the tech said, it took him just a few minutes and he was done. I finalized the arrangements for Jonny's funeral, and I advised Claire. About two hours later, she told me the body had been picked by the funeral home.

Tears came to my eyes. I sat there in silence, mourning my friend. Then the reality of his death brought me back. So many questions. Who could have done this? That was the question, in addition to who had hacked my phone and computer.

My thoughts were interrupted by a knock on the door. A well-dressed man entered. He looked like he was with a funeral home, but then he showed me his badge. He was FBI. He signaled for me to keep quiet.

--"Hi, my name is William Steward. I am here from the funeral home to make sure all the paperwork for the retrieval of the body of Jonny Price is correct," he said, approaching my desk.

--"Please come in and sit down," I said.

He handed me a note and a phone. The note said, "Call your sister and use my phone. It is secure. Also, turn off your phone and your computer, as well as your laptop.'

I did as I was told, although with some skepticism. How did I know this person in front of me as working for my sister. This could be the person that killed my friend and the art dealer.

--"Hi sis, what's up," I said, "I have the person from the funeral home you sent over. Thank you for doing this. I will call you later to tell you how it all went.... Yes, I will take care. Have a wonderful day."

I hanged up the phone and returned the phone to the man sitting in front of me. He then said, "I will be checking your computer and laptop. They are hacked, just like your phone has been hacked. I will give my report to SSA Morris, and she will get back to you. Is that okay?"

--"Yes, that will be fine," I said.

--"Then turn on your phone and talk to me as if you were

making the funeral arrangements."

I did as I was told and the conversation went on for about ten minutes, then he thanked me and left.

This was so strange, but I knew my sister had my back, and that felt really good at this time.

As I sat there looking at all the paperwork that had accumulated on my desk, Claire came in.

--"Hi there. What brings you up here," trying to fake a smile. Then I turned off my phone.

--"Why are you turning off your phone?" she asked.

--"It's been hacked," I said, annoyed.

--"I have the report on our art dealer. He had two shots to the back of the head, execution style. Ballistics determined that he was shot with the same gun that shot Price. He was kneeling at the time. There was no evidence that he was tied or duct taped and there was no evidence of torture. He was killed where we found him. There was no other trace in the area; no fingerprints, no hair, nothing. He was in good health at the time off death," she said.

--"Thank you for the information. I am going to turn on my phone and we are going to talk about the funeral," I said.

Before I was able to turn on the phone, Claire stopped me, "Could you please tell me what the hell is going on?" she asked.

--"My phone and computers are hacked. It is a very high-tech hacking. We don't know who has hacked them. Fran is looking into it, so for now, we hope that if I turn my phone off, I can avoid the hackers knowing what I am doing," I said.

--"What the hell is going on? Who do you think is behind all of this?" she asked.

--"No clue. It has to be someone very powerful and with

lots of money. This hack is very sophisticated. At this point, I don't know who to trust," I said.

--You know you can trust me; we have been friends for a long time. We have been there for each other in the good times and bad times, right," she said.

--"I know. I did not mean you. I mean within the department. So, I am turning on the phone and we are going to talk about the funeral," I said.

I turned on the phone and made an exasperated comment about how the phone must have something wrong, that it keeps on turning off, and that I might need to replace it. We both laughed and for about ten minutes talked about Jonny's funeral. Then Claire went back to her office.

CHAPTER 5

The Funeral

It was Saturday. The day woke up cloudy and cold. You could say it was a good omen for a funeral.

There were some things in life that I really hated, and HATE in capital letters; hospitals and funerals. Nothing good ever comes from either.

I was having my second cup of coffee when there was a knock on my door. I knew it was Fran and Sasha, so I told them to come in.

--"Hi sis, and good morning. Are you ready for this?" she asked.

--"As ready as I will ever be. Did you know how much I hate funerals." I said.

--"I know. By the way, Mom sends her regards," she said.

--"You know we are here for you, right?" Sasha said in a concerned tone.

After that exchange, I got ready, and we left for the funeral home.

The service for Jonny was going to be at the funeral home. Then he would be cremated and his ashes placed in a crypt and that was it. I did not expect many people. Maybe a few of his fellow grooms, the trainer at the last stable he worked and that was it.

I really did not expect anyone from the police force, outside of Peterson and her partner, and maybe Claire. And I was right about who the people that showed up. But I was surprised to see Tom.

He did not know Jonny; he only knew what I had said about him. But my question was how he knew where and when the service was going to be. I guess he read the obituary. But why? That was the question to ask.

--"Hi, I did not expect you to be here," I said as I approached him.

--"I just wanted to know how you were doing. I know how much you hate funerals," he said.

We talked for a few more minutes, then I moved to welcome the other people arriving. And just as I thought, there were the other two grooms that he worked with, the trainer, who said that the stable owner could not make it and sent his condolences, in addition to a check to help cover some of the expenses of the funeral.

I told him that there was a basket at the entrance that he could put the check there with all the other donations. He hesitated for a second and then did what I asked him.

I did not want to be seen as receiving money from maybe our prime suspect, which could be understood as a bribe. Not in the mood for that.

The service was short. I did the eulogy. One of the grooms stood up and spoke and that was it. I would say overall the service took about 30 minutes. Then Jonny's body was taken and that was it.

My heart felt so heavy. I just wanted to run from there and find a place where I could just sit and cry, but I knew that was not possible. Even though it was a Saturday, there was still work to be done.

I discreetly passed a note to Peterson that I wanted to see her at my house later on.

Then the goodbyes started, and before I knew everyone was gone, with the exception of Fran and Sasha. Claire, and Peterson. Tom had left shortly after my eulogy. Before we left, Peterson took the basket with the checks. There were just three; one from Fran and Sasha, one from Claire and one from the owner of the stables.

Not long after, we were all at my apartment. And for a brief time, we celebrated the life of a man who had a very rough life. A man who loved beer, nachos, and horses. A man who tried so hard to accomplish his dreams, but couldn't and ended up dead too early. A friend I will miss dearly.

We talked, we laughed, and I was able to finally cry, to mourn the death of someone I loved, and I will miss.

CHAPTER 6

The Investigation Continues

It was Sunday, the day following Jonny's funeral. I hoped I would be able to take some more time to mourn my friend, but I was so wrong.

About mid-day, Fran and Sasha were at my apartment and soon after Claire arrived, followed by Peterson. We all were back to work; we could not lose a beat. Fran passed a note telling all to turn off their phones. This was a precaution to make sure that we were not heard. Then we got to work.

According to Peterson, when they got to Jonny's room, it looked like someone had tossed the room. They were looking for something and it seemed that they were not able to find it. They destroyed everything. But Peterson was able to find, in the inside of one of Jonny's boots, a small flash drive. And to our advantage, whoever was there missed that. Peterson made sure that it was entered into evidence, but not before making a copy of it.

Regarding trace evidence once again, there was no trace evidence; nothing to figure out who had been in that room.

The same thing happened at the tack room; no trace evidence, but they were able to find a chair with markings that resembled scratches. Claire said she was checking the chair to see if the wood of the chair matched with the splinters found under Jonny's nails. Also, some oil was found on the floor of the tack room and Claire would try to match it to the oil found on the plastic tarp.

Fran, on the other hand, during all this exchange was working on being able to open the flash drive on her tablet. She stated that yes, my phone, and both of my computers had been hacked with a very sophisticated hack that will allow the hacker not only to hear and see what I was doing, but to also traces what I was writing. Whoever was doing the hacking had access to this equipment and definitely had some money and connections. She explained that this type of hack was too sophisticated for just your normal hacker, although she knew that there were some really great hackers out there that were capable of hacking anything. She said she and her people would continue to work on the hacker, and on the connection to me.

And by this time, she was able to open the flash drive. Jonny was able to copy documents regarding the sale and the buying of horses by the stable he worked at.

The ledger went back as far as 2012, and it seemed that the swindle to buy, sell and scam horse insurance companies was a very lucrative one.

Fran said she would take a close look at the papers from the flash drive. On the other hand, Peterson was going to continue with the investigation on Jonny's death.

I told Peterson that I was able to secure a search warrant for the trainer's office and one for the owner's offices. I knew that might be a long shot, but I was willing to take the risk.

I asked Peterson to do a background check on the owner

of the stables, as well as the trainer, and to take a close look at their finances, now that we had a check with a checking and routing number, which made it easy. Maybe too easy. I asked Peterson to take the check and enter it into evidence. If there was anything there, I did not want it linked to me.

I also asked Peterson to check on the connections between Jonny and the art gallery owner.

And just like that the meeting was over. We all turned on our phones and continued to talk as if nothing were going on. At least I tried.

It was so frustrating to be restricted on my use of my personal technology, but, on the other hand, I wanted to find out what was going on.

It was Monday morning and as always, I finished my daily run, took my shower, served me a coffee and a toasted bagel with cream cheese and jelly. I sat down to read my emails. An email from Peterson popped up as urgent. Then there it was: Another murder related to this case.

I immediately left my house and headed toward the stables. It seemed like the trainer had hanged himself.

When I arrived at the stables, Claire was already there, as well as Peterson and her partner. It was remarkably interesting that people associated with this stable were dying left and right.

--"Suicide or murder?" I asked.

--"I will not know until I get him on my table. But I would say it is questionable. If you take a look at how the rope made markings on the wood, it will reflect that the rope was thrown over the beam, not consistent with a suicide and more with a hanging. But again, I will not be sure until I do a full autopsy," Claire said.

--"Okay, anything else?" I said.

--"Once again with this hanging, there is no trace

evidence. Nothing that could show that there was anyone else here but the victim," Claire said.

--"I want this office gone through with a fine-tooth comb. I don't want a single spot missed. I want every piece of paper checked. I need to know what is going on here," I said as I walked back to my car.

Back at my office, things just went on as usual, paperwork and more paperwork. It was about 6 pm when I was able to leave the office.

Next morning, I was in the office bright and early. I wanted to get an early start on the day and maybe I might be able to go home early. But that was just a hope. As I sat there going over more paperwork, Peterson and Martinez came in.

I showed her a sign that read, "TURN OFF YOUR PHONE" as I turned off my phone.

--"What's up?" I asked.

--"Got some info about the art dealer, Mr. Brookes. First, let me tell you that Jonny had three great loves in life; he loved you, he loved horses and he loved art. All in that order. We took a closer look at Jonny's room, we found payments to Jonny from the art gallery. We also found several pencil and charcoal sketches of you and also some images of famous horses. When we checked the art gallery books, we discovered that Jonny had placed multiple pieces of art on consignment at the gallery, all of which were sold. Jonny was a very prolific artist and sold a lot of his artwork. But it was sold only by this particular art gallery," Peterson said.

--"Were you able to talk to the wife of the owner?"

--"No, she has vanished. The art gallery is closed and there is a "For Sale" sign on the door. Their bank account was cleaned out and the house has been put on sale. We talked to the real estate agent and he said he is working with her lawyer. We talked to her lawyer who stated that he could not provide any information, due to attorney-client privilege, but he did say that he had a power of attorney to sell the house, sell the business and all that was there. All proceeds were to be deposited in a bank account, but he was not able to give us the information on the bank and the account. He said that when he is able to contact Mrs. Brookes, he would inform her that we need to talk to her. So, we provided him with our business cards," she said.

--"So, she is gone. That is very convenient. If there is any new information about her husband's murder, there is no way of getting in touch with her, outside of informing her lawyer," I said.

--"Yes, and he is not willing to help," Martinez stated.

--"Also, we found out that Jonny had an apartment prior to going to work for the stables. The owner said that he left the day prior to starting to work at the stables, that he was so happy to be back to work in something he loved to do. According to the owner, Jonny was a quiet tenant, and he spent most of his time painting and sketching. He also said that the day after his body was found, two men came to the apartment and wanted to see if Jonny had left anything. They forced their way in and looked around, but the apartment was clean. They never asked if he had left anything, which he did. He gave me a flash drive; it just has a lot of photos of his artwork," Peterson said as she handed me the flash drive.

I was taken aback by the information. Then I returned the flash drive to Peterson.

--"You need to put this into evidence. I don't want someone to say we were tampering with evidence. Also, keep digging and see what you find about Mrs. Brookes and her lawyer. Anything else?" I asked.

--"Yes. We finally got the search warrant for the trainer's office and his car at the stables. We are heading that way, Chief. We are also going to try to interview the owner of the stables and, of course, the trainer," Martinez said.

--"Excellent work. Thanks and keep me posted," I said as Peterson and Martinez left my office.

I was expecting this day to be easy, but in my job, there are never easy days. I turned on my phone and continued to work.

Later, I got a call from Peterson and Martinez. They had not been gone for more than an hour. What could have happened?

--"Yes, ... what? ... Yes, keep me posted. Did you contact Claire and the Crime Scene Unit?" and with this call my day changed.

It was about 3:00 pm when Claire called me and asked if I could come down to the morgue. She had some information that she wanted to share.

As I walked in, I saw Peterson and Martinez also there.

--"What is going on?" I asked as I turned off my phone and motioned everyone to turn off theirs as well.

--"Meet Mr. William "Billy" Roger. He is the trainer at the Monroe Stables and Training. He was strangled and then he was hung to resemble a suicide. But if you take a close look at the rope markings on his neck, you can see what I am saying. Once again, there was no trace of anything at the scene; no fingerprints, no footprints, no hair, nothing. The only thing found were Mr. Roger's prints. Once again, the crime scene was clean. The only thing that we found was a note in his mouth that said "Uoytogi". You know what this means, right. Your friend "Uoytogi" is still out there and making sure you know that.

I stood there looking at the body of a healthy man, and I got angry.

--"There is this sick and perverted animal out there, killing people. I am tired of his crimes. We need to find out who he or she is and bring him to justice. This game needs to end. I need to put a stop to it as soon as possible before more people die," I firmly stated.

I continued, "Thank you, Claire. I need you to send the Crime Scene Team back to the trainer's office and go through it once again with a fine-tooth comb. No one is that perfect. They always make a mistake, and we need to find that mistake. Please keep me posted of anything else you find. Peterson and Martinez, I need you to interview the owner of the Monroe Stables and Training," I said, and then returned to my office.

My day was like many other days, buried in paperwork, with the only difference of the calls from the Chief of Police demanding that I solve the murders of Jonny, the art dealer and now the horse trainer. I tried to explain that we were working on the cases, but that did not seem to appease him. As always, our conversation ended in him threatening my job.

After conversations like this, I wondered if it had been better for me to stay as a Lieutenant or just an Inspector. But here I am, and I need to solve these murders.

I continued to work and look at all the evidence provided to me by Peterson and Martinez. One thing stood out: The murderer was a very meticulous person. He/she knew about police procedures. He/she is intelligent and likes to prove that he/she are more intelligent than the authorities. He/she exhibits psychopathic traits: He/she could show signs of antisocial behavior, narcissism, he/she could be superficially charming and, in some cases, even impulsivity.

He/she is callous and shows unemotional traits, also a lack of guilt and a complete lack of empathy. This makes he/she extremely hard to pin down in a world of horses, a world that very few people know a lot about. And entangled in this obscure world there is a psychopath. This is a great world to get lost in, but when I started to investigate some of his killings, he found me to be a great challenge. This presents a risk to me and to all those around me.

I continued working on the ton of paperwork that cluttered my desk when both Peterson and Martinez knocked on my door.

--"Got a moment Chief?" Peterson asked.

--"Yes, come on in," I said waving them in, "What's up?"

--" Mr. Alexander Monroe is gone..." she said as I interrupted her.

--"What do you mean? Is he dead?" I asked.

--"No. He's gone. The owner of Monroe Stables and Training is gone. He has vanished, along with his family, just like the art gallery owner's wife. And I bet you can't guess who his lawyer is?"

--"You know I'm no good at this guessing game," I said.

--"The same lawyer as the widow of the art gallery owner. He is handling the sale of the stable. This is according to the house caretaker," she said.

--"I spoke to the only groom that was left at the stables. He said he had been paid, as well as another groom. He also said that all the horses were taken away, but he did not know where. He also said he was the one that found the dead trainer, and before he could call the police, we were there," Martinez said.

--"So, anyone that could give us some information on what is going on at those stables is either gone or dead. Very convenient," I said, "I will get you a search warrant for the house. Go through it with a fine-tooth comb. There has to be something there that could help us find out who is behind all this. Then talk to the lawyer. I know that will be a waste of time, but I still want to see if he is willing to provide any information. Did the house caretaker provide any information on what happened to the Monroe family?" I asked.

--"Yes. She said she believes they left last night. She believes that the family packed everything they could. The safe was left open and empty. It looked like they just got up and left. There was a note on the dining room table with money to pay the employees and the grooms and instructions to get in touch with the lawyer, who was going to be handling everything else. There were also letters of recommendations for all employees," Peterson said.

--"Did she know about the trainer being dead?" I asked.

--"No. She was surprised to find out. She thought he would have been gone also," Peterson replied.

--"Anything else?" I asked.

--"Yes. She said that she had seen a lot of movement at the stables in the last few days. She saw two new men at the stables moving horses into trailers. She had never seen those guys before. According to her, they seem to be Hispanic, and they spoke Spanish. She did not know what they were saying because she doesn't speak Spanish, but she knew they were in a rush to get the horses gone," Martinez said.

--"How did she know the men were Hispanic? The house is far from the stables." I asked.

--"She said she would take food to the trainer at the same time every day. When she took him food the last time, she saw them, and she heard them. She said that Billy told her to get back to the house and forget what she had seen. The next thing she knew, the police found Billy dead," Peterson stated.

--"Ok, get search warrants for the house and the property. We need that property completely checked. Take ground penetrating equipment and anything else you might need. We need to find out what went on at that property. In addition to that, we need to find out where the owner of the stable and his family are. We need to get subpoenas for their bank accounts and credit history and anything and everything that could lead us to where they are," I said.

Both Peterson and Martinez got up and left my office. I found the information they provided interesting. Hopefully the search of the property would provide something useful in solving the crimes at hand.

Two hours had not gone by, when the Chief of Police called me. He was irate. I had never heard him so upset in my life. He was ordering me to turn on the TV. And there on the news was Lt. Parks. He was giving an interview to the local television station. He was providing some of the information that just a few hours earlier Peterson and Martinez had provided me.

I could see why the Chief of Police was so angry. I was just as angry, if not more. This information was not for public consumption, not until we were ready. And the information was supposed to go through the Media Relations Officer.

I told the Chief of Police I was going to take care of it. I had just hanged up with the Chief of Police when Paul Johnson, Chief of Media Relations, walked in. He was also extremely angry. It took all I had to calm him down and I promised to take care of the matter.

I was getting so tired of Parks and his defiance of my orders. He was more than just a loose cannon; he was becoming a menace to our investigation and that needed to stop immediately.

I asked Paul and Jones Stevenson, Internal Affairs, to

come to my office. I needed guidance on what to do with Parks. I needed to put a stop to what was going on, but I needed to make sure that I did everything by the book. I did not what any further problems.

After a long meeting, it was agreed that Parks was going to be placed on a week's suspension, with no pay, as a result of disobeying a direct order. It was also agreed that after his return, if he continued to approach the press without authorization, then he was going to be brought up on charges with the possibility of permanent suspension.

Before I talked to Parks, I ran my decision past the Chief to make sure he was okay with the action. Knowing the man, I really did not want to have him change is mind later on. But he was onboard with it, and I proceeded to call Parks to my office.

When Parks entered my office, his attitude was, as always, arrogant and defiant. He walked in and sat down without even being asked.

--"I know why you asked me to come and have this little chat with you. You are upset because I told the press what was going on with the "Horse" case, but they approached me, and I believe the public needs to know." he said in a condescending tone.

--"Stand up. I didn't tell you to sit down," I said in a very stern tone and waited for him to stand up. Then I stood up and we were eye to eye. He could definitely read the anger in my eyes, and for first time, I could read some fear in his eyes.

--"I told you and I ordered you to stay away from the press, that it was the job of the Chief of the Media Relations Unit to get in touch with the press. All you had to do when they approached you was to direct them to Media Relations. But no, you had to try and undermine all of us. And this stops right now. As of NOW, you are suspended without pay for a week, and when you come back, if you have not adjusted your attitude, you will be immediately and permanently suspended from the force," I said.

--"You cannot to that. I will complain to the Chief," he said.

--"The Chief is onboard with the decision. You just compromised one of our most important cases. The mayor is on the Chief's back. You gave up our case and people involved in this case are disappearing. After you spoke out of order, what do you think was going to happen. Did you expect the Chief to give you a medal? What were you thinking? No, excuse me, you were not thinking? You wanted to show me up. You wanted everyone to think you were the greatest and I was just a mere little woman who did not know what she was doing. Well, it turns out that you were wrong. Now go, and I will see you in a week and I hope with a better attitude," I said in the roughest and angriest tone I had ever used in my life. I was hoping that this would put an end to all this intrusion, but I was totally mistaken. Within seconds, I got a text:

"Well done, but that is not going to solve your problems. There is more ahead. Be prepared. Your friend, UOYTOGI ☺ ☺ ☺ "

I could not believe this. I had forgotten to turn off the phone and he, whoever he or she was, now knew what was going on. I truly need to find this person and put an end to all this madness before more people get hurt.

CHAPTER 8

The FBI

The last thing I needed on this long day was a text from my sister, the FBI agent, asking me if I, Peterson, and Martinez could be at her office at 5:30 today. She said that she had some particularly essential information to share with us regarding the case. I texted her back that we would be there and proceeded to contact Peterson and Martinez.

At 5:30 sharp, we were all at Fran's office. We were joined by Felix Strong, Chief investigator with the Horse Insurance Industry, Keenan Armstrong, Animal Control Customs Agent, Antoinette Henderson, Fraud FBI Agent and Keith Waxman, Assistant Special Agent, Criminal Unit FBI.

After the compulsory introductions we sat down to work. First at bat was Felix Strong:

--" In case you guys did not know, Horse insurance is something very important for those people who own horses. These policies, the same as with humans, cover emergency medical care for your horse, also paying a percentage of the horse's value if the horse dies unexpectedly. One of the most important things of these policies is for those owners that use horses for breeding or racing. It is very important to remember that when you own a racing or breeding horse, whose value could be over ten thousand, it becomes even more important to have the appropriate insurance coverage in place. There are many things that are important in these policies, not only the medical coverage, but also the loss of use coverage policy, which pays the owner of the horse when the horse can no longer perform the income-producing activities, such as racing or breeding. One last thing to remember is that most horse insurance companies offer full mortality policies and limited mortality policies. Full mortality policies are used to pay the full value of the horse. On the other hand, the limited mortality policies cover a percentage of the horse's value," he explained. Then he continued, "I could see in your faces that you are wondering what all this has to do with your cases, but it is very important if you want to understand what is going on."

I looked at Fran, a bit confused, then she said, "Let's listen to what he has to say, and we will go from there.

Strong continued, "The Monroe Stables filed for payment on their mortality policies for four dead horses in the last year for a total of about $1,000,000.00. Which, in the larger scheme of things, is not a lot, but in the last five years Monroe Stables have filed an exceptionally large amount of claims on mortality insurance on their horses, most due to colic." He provided a complete graph on the death of the horses. Then he continued, "We all have heard of children having colic. Well horses do too and colic in horses remains a major cause of sickness and death, for horses. As you can see in the graph, approximately 10 percent of all horses suffer at least one bout of colic during their lifetimes, and about 6 percent of those horses die. Monroe Stables had twice as many of their horses die from colic, as well as other diseases or injuries. This raised a red flag for us…"

AND THE STORY CONTINUES

I interrupted and asked him to explain colic in horses. This was something that Jonny had mentioned in his has letter to me.

--"Colic is the leading cause of death in horses. The textbook explanation for colic is abdominal pain. This is a symptom, not a diagnosis. Some causes of colic are improper care, diet, and management practices, but colic can be prevented," he said and then continued, "When we examined the dead horses at Monroe Stables, we noticed that all the horses had been brought here from Mexico and all showed signs of previous problems with colic..." It was Peterson that interrupted this time.

--"But I thought all animals entering the USA from a foreign country have to be checked and quarantined to make sure they are healthy?" she asked.

Keenan Armstrong, Animal Control Customs Agent, answered, "You are right, and we would expect it to be that way, had the agent and veterinarian in charge at the border not been corrupt and in the pocket of this organization."

--"I am having problems understanding. Border Patrol stops people coming in from Mexico, but they just forget to check animals entering?" Martinez cynically asked.

--"You have the right to be cynical, but the procedure for the entry of horses in particular was breached. You see, the Border Patrol Agent was notified when the horses were coming in. It was usually not more than three horses, so as not to attract attention. The agent called the specific vet who inspected the horses and gave them a clean bill of health and was supposed to take them to quarantine. Meanwhile, the agent checked all the paperwork, which seemed correct. The horses then went with the vet who, instead of putting them in quarantine, turned them over to the Monroe Stable people. As soon as the horses got to the stables, they were insured and shortly after they were spread throughout the West Coast. Those that stayed at the stable died of colic or other injuries. It has taken us a long time to be able to unravel this web," Armstrong concluded.

Felix Strong interrupted, "The horses were brought in Mexico for double and triple their value. Once they arrived at the Monroe Stables, they were insured for the final value, so as not to raise suspicion. Then the horses Monroe Stable was not going to keep were sold in a private sale for four to five time their value. Monroe Stables made a lot of money. The ones they kept later died from colic or injury at the stable or at the track. Very few ever raced or were used to breed."

I interrupted, "How did you find out about this?"

--"Your friend Price contacted us and provided the information; he was about to testify when he was found dead," Strong said.

At which time Antoinette Henderson, FBI Fraud Agent, said, "This is not the first time there has been a horse fraud case. In the 70's, there was a case known as "The Horse Murders Scandal". It referred to a very large case of horse insurance fraud in the United States, at least until now. That case dealt with expensive horses, many of them show jumpers/equestrian. These very expensive horses were insured against death, accident, or disease, and then killed to collect the insurance money," she said.

--"It is not known how many horses were killed between the mid-1970s and the mid-1990s," Strong said.

--"An FBI investigation brought the horse killings to light, but the number of horses killed at the time was thought to be well over 50. Some believe that it might have been as high as one hundred," Henderson said.

--" The case was brought to light on February 17, 1977. This was due to the disappearance of Helen Vorhees Brach.

Brach, who was the widow of E. J. Brach, the founder of the E. J. Brach & Sons Candy Company, was the founder and creator of the Helen V. Brach Foundation to promote animal welfare, this was before she disappeared...." Henderson was explaining when I once again interrupted.

--"What led to her disappearance and was she ever found?" I asked.

--"No," Waxman, Fran's Assistant Special Agent, jumped in, "Helen Brach disappeared and law enforcement, yes we at the FBI, believed she was murdered by the perpetrators of the crimes. It is believed that she threatened to report their criminal activity to authorities."

--"The investigations into Brach's disappearances began to uncover an exceptionally large horse insurance fraud. At the time, and still today, the scandal was called "one of the biggest, most gruesome stories in sports" and also is considered "the biggest scandal in the history of equestrian sports," Strong said.

--According to our record, thirty-six people were indicted. They were tried for insurance fraud, mail and wire fraud, obstruction of justice, extortion, racketeering, and animal cruelty in connection with the horse murders," Waxman stated.

--"Was the murder of Brach ever solved?" Peterson asked.

--"No. The disappearance and murder of Helen Brach was never fully solved, although one man, Richard Bailey, was sentenced to 38 years and was released in 2019," Waxman stated, then continued, "This conspiracy took place over a 20-year period. During the time that the horses were murdered, the FBI, with the help of the insurance investigators, discovered several reasons that led horse owners and trainers, as well as very affluent and well-respected people, to become involved in this widespread conspiracy."

In the back of my head I thought this is turning to be like a book report. Just give me the Cliffs Notes and let's move on to how this case is relevant to our case right now.

It seemed that Fran saw my desperation and chimed in, "I know that this has become very tedious, and maybe we might have been able to give you a report, which you will get shortly, but to be able to understand our current case, we have to understand what has happened before. How about if we take a break and have some coffee."

As I was getting some coffee, Strong approached me, "I know this is a lot to absorb right now, but your case is looking very much like the case in the 70's. Many people don't have any idea of cases like this. They just see pretty horses and fast horses, but there is a lot of money behind the scenes and a lot of cruelty toward those beautiful creatures. You see, in those cases, the owner of a promising, or even prize-winning, horse was strapped for cash and decided to kill the animal to collect the insurance. I know you have come across this motive before."

--"Oh yes. The need for money is always a motive," I said.

--"Cream and sugar?"

--"What?" I asked as I looked at him.

--"Do you want cream and sugar in your coffee?" he asked.

--"No, thanks. I take my coffee black," I said.

As we walked back to the conference table, he continued to explain things.

"You should realize that something else that took place during those times is resounding in your case right now, and went beyond insurance fraud. That was the element of racketeering," Strong said.

--"Explain?" I asked.

--"This last part of the scheme consisted of taking money from very wealthy widows, by encouraging them to invest in horses. As in your case, the animals were usually over-valued or under-performing. Then the conspirators killed the animals in order to prevent the owners from uncovering how much they were taken for," he said and paused for a few seconds, then he continued, "In some cases, before these wealthy women invested, these non-performing animals were first "bid up" in value by the co-conspirators, in an attempt to make them seem more desirable to the purchasers. When the wealthy women began to suspect that the horses they had purchased had no real value, the horses would be killed for the insurance money," Strong said.

Our meeting continued for another hour with more information being provided by Strong, Armstrong, Henderson, and Waxman. Then Peterson and Martinez updated the group on what was going on with the murder cases. After all the updates and conversation, it was established that all of us would work together to solve what seemed to be a remarkably interesting case.

It was about 9:00 pm when the meeting was over, and everyone was ready to leave when Fran asked me to stay a bit longer. I was so tiered, and my first instinct was to say no, but I obliged.

--"What do you know about Tom?" she asked.

--"I was married to the guy for six years and he is still my friend. Why?" I asked.

--"I have obtained some information about him that I think you really need to know," she said.

--"What information?" I asked.

There was a long pause, then she handed me a folder

marked secret. In it there was a dossier on Thomas "Tom" Hogan. The dossier was quite extensive and detailed. I looked at Fran with a questioning look.

--"I know you are wondering why I did this. To tell you the truth, it was a gut feeling and I always go with my gut feeling," she said, then continued, Tom is Uoytogi."

I looked at her with surprise, "Tom, my Tom, are you crazy?" I said.

She looked at me worried, but at the same time hurt. It was obvious this was not easy for her; it was not easy for me either. But here we were, the two of us.

--"Please listen to me," she said, then continued, "I found it strange that after Tom's visit to your apartment after Jonny's death and the flowers, a very sophisticated bug was found on your phone, as well as mine and Sasha's. The only person who had access to those phones at the same time was Tom. So I had a full background check done on him. Sorry, but I just needed to know." She said, then she continued, "As you see, Tom was a CIA agent. His cover was as an antique dealer. According to the information obtained, he went rough times about ten years ago. But as you know, once a CIA agent, always a CIA agent. In the file, there is information on when you got married and divorced. No, I was not running a background check on you. You just happened to be there because you were married to the man. During his time with the CIA, he was connected to some very disreputable people. He disappeared for about 6 years, which is the time it is believed he was with you. Then he appeared again. This time he is linked to a large smuggling cartel from Mexico."

--"Fran, this is ridiculously hard to believe. Tom is a good guy. He has always been a good guy. I was at his warehouse. Don't you think that if he were doing something illegal, I would have known about it. This is simply wrong and offensive. My own sister doing a background check on me and my ex-husband. I can't believe this," I said in an angry tone.

--"I know you're upset, and I do understand how you feel, but please read the dossier. After you are done, we can talk. Please, I ask you to trust me on this one. I know it is asking a lot from you. We barely know each other, but I do want the best for you. Please, I ask you to trust me," She pleaded.

I stormed out of her office, dossier in hand and headed home. During the whole ride home, I was wondering if, in reality, I knew both of these people. Fran I had just met, and she definitely was my sister by blood, but we did not have that sister relationship that you develop with familiarity and everyday contact.

Tom, on the other hand, had been my husband. We shared so much. He was there when my father died. He held my hand, he helped me with my grief. How could I have been so wrong about him, if this dossier was right. How could I have not seen the signs, if this dossier is right. But maybe I did see the signs and I just did not want to accept them. Love sometimes blinds you to the reality that is right in front of you.

I knew that Tom traveled a lot for his business, but he never invited me on his trips. He always blamed it on my job. I was too busy to take time with him. Now looking back, it seems like it was he who just did not want me to travel with him.

I remember the night my father died. I just could not get in touch with him. The phone he gave me went always to voicemail and I just could not get him at the hotel. It took two days. When he called me, he explained that he had lost his phone and that the hotel forgot to give him my messages. He told me he was on the next flight back.

I also remember his insistence for me to be behind a desk. He thought it was better and that I would make a good supervisor. Maybe he wanted me behind the desk so I would not find out who he really was.

I felt so confused. Here I am doubting a man I have known for many years and accepting the ideas of a woman I have known for just a few years. I need to talk to someone, but who. Tom. NO, that will not work this time. Maybe Claire. I will call her as soon I get home.

I did not have time to call anyone. Within minutes of arriving at my house, there was a knock on the door. It was Tom. I hesitated to open the door, but if I did not, he would know that there was something wrong so, I opened the door.

--"Hi there, what brings you by?" I asked at the door.

--"Can I come in?" he asked.

--"Sure, come on in," I said.

I was totally unsure of what was going to happen. I just hoped that nothing would happen and that we would have a good, civil conversation, as always.

--"So, what brings you by?" I asked.

--"I have been trying to get in touch with you the last few days, but my calls go straight to voice mail. I was worried. Are you ok?" he said as he sat down on the couch close to the door. I felt like he was blocking my exit, but I did not show it.

--"Nothing is going on, other than I am having problems with my phone. I have asked the department for a new one, but they are taking their sweet time," I said.

--"I was just worried, you always answer all my calls, and I thought something was wrong, that is all. Are you doing, okay? How is the Jonny case doing?" he asked.

--"All is well." I said and I asked him if he wanted something to drink. I told him I had just discovered a new wine with a chocolate taste that I knew he would like. He agreed and we sat to a bottle of chocolate wine, for a few hours. We talked about many things nothing to do with my work, my investigation, just mundane things. After a few hours he left, and I wondered what he was really after.

Things did not feel right between him and I anymore. But before I could make whatever that was right, I really needed to read the file that Fran had given me. But before I did that, I needed to make sure my phone was off as well as my computer. I even became paranoid and thought that maybe my television set was bugged. So, I went to the only room in my apartment that I felt safe, the bathroom. I sat down on the floor and read the whole file. Then things began to make sense of my life with Tom. How could I have been so stupid not to realize who and what he was. What kind of investigator was I? Love does make you see what you want to see and not the reality of things. Yes, Fran was right; Tom was the enemy. So, where do we go from here.

After reading and re-reading the file several times to make sure I was not rushing things, I decided to go to sleep. I would call Fran in the morning and see what we are going to do.

I didn't sleep at all. Everything seemed to be coming back to my mind. First thing in the morning I called Fran. We agreed to meet at her office for lunch. I knew it was going to be a long morning, but I also knew I had to make the best of the morning.

CHAPTER 9

TOM?

It was noon when I arrived at Fran's office. As always, I had to go through the checkpoint, show my badge, and my gun. Then they called Fran and she came to the checkpoint and got me. This was the usual routine. I believe it would be almost impossible for anyone to get in without being checked.

When we got to her office, I jokingly asked her, "Are we going to use the cone of silence?" That was the best I could do with truly little sleep.

She did not seem amused. There was a very heavy silence between us and I really felt uncomfortable, but I guess this was something that was not going to be resolved with a "Get Smart" joke.

When we got to her office, and she motioned me to close the door and then sit.

--"I read your file. I still have problems with it, but this file answers a lot of questions I always had," I said in an incredibly sad tone.

--"I am so sorry Jane. The last thing I wanted to do was bring you pain, but it was important for you to know, for your own sake and for the case," she said. Then she added,

"No, I did not do this for the case. I started doing it for your safety and then it boiled down to the case. All the evidence leads to Tom and, believe me, it bothered me to realize that he was the head of the organization," she said.

--"What led you to go that way?" I asked.

--"Insignificant things. To start with, the day Jonny died and the flowers and the following day, the death of the art gallery owner. Things did not feel right. Then I found out that the bug in our phones was very sophisticated and only a person with international and powerful connections could get their hands on that type of bug," she said.

--"I still don't understand, why Tom?" I asked.

--"Because outside of us that night, Tom was the only one there, so I started to look into his background. Then the flash drive that Peterson and Martinez found in Jonny's boot, and you gave to me, provided more information on the organization…" she said, as I interrupted.

--"I don't understand," I said.

--"The flash drive that Jonny had in his boot, and in the painting, provided an unbelievably detailed information on the organization, which was what killed him. Had he not found out and copied all the information, he would still be alive. But his love for horses and his love for you led him to dig in deeper and deeper. He was almost at the point of discovering who the head of the organization was," she said.

--"But how did you come up with Tom?" I asked.

--"It was not easy, but there was one thing that I learned as an investigator; follow the money, and the money led me to Tom. His dealings, his travels. Every time there was a horse delivery, it was right after Tom visited Mexico. At the same time, there was a large amount of money deposited in his offshore account. Also, he was a friend of the owner of the stable and the lawyer that represents both the stable owner and the wife of the art dealer," she said.

--"By your logic, that should also make me his accomplice," I said sarcastically.

--"You don't have an offshore account," she said, with a smile on her face.

--"As far as you know...Did you check?" I asked.

--"What do you think?" she said.

--"Might as well leave that unanswered," I said.

--"It took a lot of digging, but we were able to put it all together," she said.

--"So, the dog and pony show last night was for my benefit, right, because all that information could be found on the internet. There was nothing really secret or confidential on all that information," I said.

--"No, it wasn't just for you. It was also for the one hearing our conversation," she said.

--"You mean Tom, right. He was at my house last night as soon as I got there," I said.

--"I know."

--"You had me tailed?" I asked, terribly upset.

--"Yes, not because I doubted you, but because I was worried," she stated.

--"Why? Because you did not trust me, because you thought I was involved with Tom in this scheme? Why, sister why?" I said in a truly angry tone.

--"No, I was just worried about you and your safety," she stated.

--"And now, what are we going to do?" I asked.

--"Well, we found a way to block the bug, at least temporarily, which is good. Now we have to set a plan to be able to catch him, and I need your help. Do I have your help?" she stated.

I hesitated a few minutes. This was Tom, the man I had married, the man I had trusted for so many years. It was so hard to believe that he might be involved in something so dirty, but I had to do the right thing, if nothing else, to show that Tom was innocent of what he was being accused.

--"Yes, I will help. What do I have to do?" I asked.

--"Let's go to the outer office. There is no "cone of silence" there," she said with a smile.

We sat at a desk close to a window to talk. She said that she needed me to call Tom and ask him to meet with me at the restaurant where he asked me to marry him. She explained that I would be wired and that she was sure that I knew what I needed to do to make sure that he admitted to running the organization and that he had ordered the death of both Jonny and the art dealer, as well as the disappearance of the art dealer's wife and the owner of the stables and his family.

All this was so hard to swallow, but I knew I had to do it and I agreed. She asked me to call Tom right there, and to use my phone. I believed, and I was almost sure that she believed, that if he had such a sophisticated bugging system, he would be able to know that I was calling from the FBI office. But I followed the plan, and Tom and I set a date for that night at our favorite restaurant. All was set, and I left Fran's office as soon as I could. I just felt bad about everything, but I needed to know the truth. If Tom was behind the death of Jonny, he had to pay for his crimes.

About an hour after I had left Fran's office, Tom was standing in front of Fran's desk. This was something that Fran was expecting. Tom came straight to her office. He did not go through the checkpoint, he had all the security he needed to avoid the checkpoint.

--"Hi Tom. I was waiting for you. What took you so

long?" she said, as she hit the silent alarm in her desk.

--"I gathered you would be waiting for me. You are a very smart woman, but maybe not as smart as you think. I hope you understand that as we talk, there is someone in both your house and Jane's house, waiting for both Jane and Sasha and they will both be killed as they enter their houses," he said as he sat in front of her.

--"You know Tom, you should have sent a better assassin to kill me. If he had been a better assassin, you would not be in this predicament," she said.

--"Yes, you are right, but I discovered that you girls are ridiculously hard to kill. I tried, but I totally failed, didn't I? But I don't think I will this time. And I will kill you right here in your own office. I will walk out of here and no one will be the wiser that I killed you. You are here alone, and that makes it so much better," he said with a smile.

--"Before you kill me, I have a few questions for you. When did you know that Jane and I were sisters?" she asked.

--"I saw you at Quantico. I thought for a second it was Jane. Then I found out who you were. I did a complete background on you and your wife. I found out that your mother's doctor was related to Jane's mother. Then when Jane's father died, I found a letter that explained everything, so I took advantage of the situation. I followed your career in the FBI and when the time was right, I inserted influence to have you moved here to San Francisco..."

"So, you wanted me killed, here in Jane's territory, and for her to find out that the dead woman was her sister. That would have devastated her, and she would probably not even able to follow through with the case. Right?" she said.

--"Exceptionally good, but you did not die. Then I tried killing her, but the idiot used a knife instead of a gun and she did not die. Like I said before, you guys are really hard to kill. But this time, I will not fail. Everything is set. I will be able to continue with my business. You know this is a very lucrative business," he said.

--"Yes, but what about the other agents involved in the investigation. Are you going to kill them all?" she asked.

--"Oh, they will all die, in some form or the other. You can count on that," he said with a snicker, "Now my dear Fran, prepare to die. This is your time, and I am so happy I will be the one doing it," he said.

--"You know Tom, I don't think so. I really don't think that you will be able to kill me, because, as you so eloquently said, we are awfully hard to kill. I was waiting for your visit, so I made sure that I was the only one in the office so you could feel confident in your ability to kill me, but I had a silent alarm installed. I hit it the moment you walked in. Also, I advised everyone on the security staff to be on the lookout for you. The security cameras around the building captured you when you came in. We have you on the stairs leading to this floor and entering the office. You are such a narcissist that you thought you could pull this off, but you won't get the job done. You might shoot me, but you are not getting out of here alive. So, you have two options: You can turn yourself in, or you can die in the process. It is all up to you," she said.

As she spoke, the door opened and two FBI agents with guns drawn walked in. Tom looked at her and knew he had been beaten.

--"I might not have been able to kill you but, at this time both Jane and Sasha are dead," he said in a very arrogant voice.

--"Wrong again. Both Jane's apartment and my house have been under surveillance, and your men have been apprehended. Both Jane and Sasha are safe and are under protective custody. You lose once again. This is the end of the road for you and your organization," she said.

Tom gave up without a struggle. He knew that he had been beaten, and as he was being handcuffed, he laughed, "I should have known better," he finally said.

As Fran had said, the man in Jane's apartment, waiting for her, was arrested along with his accomplice as they tried to enter her apartment. The apartment was thoroughly searched for anyone else before she was allowed to enter. The same thing with Sasha and Fran's house.

During the search of both the apartment and the house, multiple bugs were found, and all the phones were cleared of the any trace bugs.

All this process took sometime, but also the search of Tom's apartment and warehouse revealed that Lieutenant Parks was on Tom's payroll, as well as several Customs Agents and several veterinarians. The organization expanded from San Diego all the way to Washington State. The evidence collection took months to collect, but at the end, it was all worth it.

During all the time that the investigation took place, I found myself also under investigation, both by the FBI and Internal Affairs. My ex-husband and a Lieutenant under my command were involved in a RICO case. So, for weeks I was home going crazy and even paranoid.

It was during this time that Claire called.

--"Hi there... No, my friend, I am not doing anything tonight... I really would not be good company.... Why, do I have to list things for you...Really not good company.... You have pizza and wine...Okay I will see you shortly," went the conversation.

And about five minutes later the doorbell rang and there was Claire, pizza and our favorite wine in hand.

--"You took so long; traffic," I said in a joking voice.

--"SO, how are you doing?" she immediately asked. Claire was not one to beat around the bush.

--"Doing fine," I said as I got plates for the pizza, and she uncorked the wine.

--"Don't lie to me. I've known you for a long time. Come on, how are you doing, really," she said, in a soft tone.

--"What do you want me to tell you? That I don't trust myself and those around me. That the man that was my husband and my friend was one of the world's greatest criminals. That a Lieutenant under my command was also a criminal. That I was under investigation and that my whole life has been a lie. Ohhh, what else, that the two people that I loved and admired, sarcastic and angry tone.

--"I am here for you, my friend. I have always been here for you," she said.

--"I know. It's just that it is so hard to deal with all this. For many years I thought no I believed I was a good cop. Then one day you wake up and find out that you were taken for a fool by people you trusted," I said.

--"You know that this to will pass. Any idea when they plan to reinstate you," she said.

--"Yes, I know. I just got the letter of reinstatement. I can go back to work next week," I said.

--"Are you planning on going back?" she asked.

--"I really don't know," I said as I took a slice of pizza.

And the rest of the evening went on with more silent moments than conversation, but just the fact that I had someone in my corner made things just a bit easier.

CHAPTER 10

The End, Maybe?

It had been about a year since the arrest of Tom, his accomplices, and the start of the trial.

So many things have changed in that year. Tom was charged in Federal Court with RICO charges.

His two accomplices were charged by the San Francisco District Attorney for the murder of Jonny, the murder of the art dealer, the murder of the trainer and the attempt on my life and Sasha's life.

According to Tom's two accomplices, and the deal they agreed to, they said it was Tom who ordered the murder of Jonny, once he realized that Jonny had obtained information on his organization. He then ordered them to dump the body at the SFPDHQ just to make sure I hurt, because he knew how important Jonny was to me. They also stated that they killed the art dealer as they were searching the house for anything related to Jonny. They knew through Tom that Jonny sold his artwork only to this particular art dealer for years, so if Jonny had hidden anything of value to give to me, the art dealer would have it. But because the police arrived too soon, they were not able to find the painting of me with the original information on Tom's organization, and thanks to that information the federal agencies could make the RICO case against Tom.

Tom's two accomplices testified that Tom told them to kill the trainer, because he let Jonny steal the information on his organization. This was to be a message to the rest of the organization to be careful; sloppy work would get you kill.

But Tom's accomplices had no idea where the art dealer's wife was nor where Monroe, the owner of the stables, and his family were. I believe that part of the case will go down the same way the Helen Vorhees Brach disappearance went down.

Finally, they also confessed to Tom's order to kill me and Sasha as he took care of Fran. It seemed like all loose ends were tied up. Nothing else was left to do on the case other than wait for the trial.

In the meantime, I had become very reclusive. I did not know who to trust. I had lost confidence in myself; it was hard going to work every day and looking at my fellow officers who had lost their trust in me.

But through all this, it seemed like the only person I could trust was Claire. I found myself barely getting in touch with Fran and Sasha. I missed them so much, but I did not know what to do. They knew I had been married to one of the world's biggest criminals and I did not know that. He had ordered the murder of my friend, my sister, my sister's wife, and me. And yet, until that day, I was trying to find some redeeming quality in this man. What a fool I was.

Then, as I sat there in my living room, having wine and a pizza, feeling sorry for myself, there was a knock on the door. As I opened it, to my surprise it was Fran and Sasha.

--"We are coming in," Sasha said.

--"Sure," I said.

I was glad and nervous to see them. I had missed them.

--"You know I am tired of you moping around. You did not do anything wrong. It is time for you to get out of this self-imposed isolation and get back to living. There is a lot to do, and in the last few months your detectives have done some really excellent work. Come on, let's put this behind us. And just in case you need some incentive, Sasha and I have some incredibly happy news to share with you. We are expecting a baby girl. And Frances Jane needs an aunt to guide her. What do you think, can you do that?" Fran said.

This was a very happy moment for all. It was really time for all of us to move forward. This nightmare was over. I had a family that needed me, and I needed. I know it was going to take some time to heal all the wounds, but a new life was arriving for the family and that was a sign of the future.

Mr. Uoytogi was gone forever from our lives, and I was going to be okay.

www.ingramcontent.com/pod-product-compliance
Lightning Source LLC
LaVergne TN
LVHW041540060526
838200LV00037B/1065